BOOKS for BOYS

The Knights of the Brown Table

IAN WHYBROW
ILLUSTRATED BY TONY ROSS

Hodder Children's Books

A division of Hachette Children

D1077624

**For Pat and Dave Steele of Newton House,
North Elmham, and all their little treasures.**

Text copyright © 2006 Ian Whybrow
Illustrations copyright © 2006 Tony Ross
First published in Great Britain in 2006
by Hodder Children's Books

The rights of Ian Whybrow and Tony Ross to be identified as the Author and
Illustrator of the Work have been asserted by them in accordance with the
Copyright, Designs and Patents Act 1988.

2

A Catalogue record for this book is available
from the British Library

ISBN-10: 0 340 91113 1
ISBN-13: 978 0 340 91113 6

Printed and bound in Great Britain by
Bookmarque Ltd, Croydon, Surrey

The paper and board used in this paperback by
Hodder Children's Books are natural recyclable products made from
wood grown in sustainable forests. The manufacturing processes conform
to the environmental regulations of the country of origin.

Hodder Children's Books
a division of Hodder Headline Limited
338 Euston Road
London NW1 3BH

The Coming of the Table

I'm not going to say it was *all* Max's
fault. True, Mr Bartrum had it in for
us, and he's Lord Almeley's gamekeeper, so that was double trouble.
Still, it's always fun blaming Max.

We were standing round this old
table. Max had just dragged it all the
way to our fortress from outside
Mr Bartrum's cottage. I said, "Max,
you're such a derr! You can't go
around stealing tables off people!

3

No wonder Mr Bartrum went bonkers!"

Poor old Max. He was so hot and bothered, he was gasping like Miss Harris's bulldog and he looked

as if his freckles were going to explode. Wearing a knight's helmet, chain-mail, breastplate and surcoat didn't help. OK, they were mostly plastic but still hot. "I keep tellin' you! I never *stole* this table! I *found* it. It was left in a skip outside his house! It was going to the dump!"

We were in our fortress in Batch Wood. It was a tool shed before Thurston's dad got rid of it to make room for a hot tub. We put it on top of this manmade mound like a huge molehill. On the map, they call it *The Twt*. (If you can't speak Welsh, you say it like *foot* only you start with a T.) They say it was built by the ancient Brits to make sure the Welsh weren't coming to attack.

You could see miles across the hills if it wasn't for the trees in the way.

We had a notice on the door with a double meaning saying *Keep! Out!* Because you can have *Keep* like the keep of a castle and *Out* meaning *Not in here*. And if you were a bit thick, it just meant *Go away*. It was better than boiling oil for keeping out invaders.

It was holiday time and we were having our knights-in-armour craze. Max thought having a table would make us like King Arthur's mates.

I said, "But Max, this isn't even a *round* table. This is a kitchen table."

"What are you *talkin'* about?" he answered. "It's brown! Haven't you heard of King Alfred and the

Knights of the Brown Table?"

What could we say? How can anybody be that SAD?

Knights are supposed to get roast venison for lunch but Thurston was making us marmalade, squirty cheese and cold baked bean sandwiches. Max likes marmalade, I like squirty cheese and Thurston likes baked beans. But Thurston, being so bossy, he said it was a waste of time doing separate fillings. So he was slapping all the stuff in together between the slices of bread.

Me and Max were too hungry to care. We held our hands out.

Thurston handed me a sandwich but kept Max's behind his back. "You could be lying about this table," he said. "I think we'd better have a Trial by Ordeal." He waved the sandwich under Max's nose and started whispering like a hypnotist. "If you pinched Mr Bartrum's table, you will get into a temper and your sandwich will disappear." He took a bite out of it.

"Hoy!" yelled Max. "Eat your own!"

"Told you!" crowed Thurston. "Now, looketh deep into my eyes and telleth me that thou art not telling whoppers unto this court."

"What court?" yelled Max.
"Gimme that sandwich!" He grabbed
Thurston round the neck and
bundled him on to the floor.

Sniff was lying under the table
that Max had "found". He woke up
as soon as the fight started. He likes
fights. He jumped on top of them,

growling and scrabbling at them with his great hairy paws.

"Ow! Gerrrim off!" yelled Max and Thurston.

"Don't blame my faithful hound," I said. "You know he always goes mad if you start flapping about. He's the same at home with the hoover."

"Raaaalph!" agreed Sniff. Then he smelt the sandwich that Thurston was holding above his head. SHHHLOPPP! Gone.

All Kitted Up

Max was well angry. He only calmed down when I gave him double rations. Thurston made sure Max's mouth was too full to answer back before he had another go at him. "Well you should ask permission before you go taking stuff out of skips! You know Mr Bartrum hates you."

"He can't take a joke, that's all!" blurted Max, spraying us with crumbs.

"Just because I said *Hello Mister Bedroom* to him outside the vet's. He was taking his cat for a check-up or somefink."

"Yes, well he works for a Lord!" said Thurston, pointing his finger. "He thinks he's above common ginger oiks like you!"

"Who are you callin' ginger?" yelled Max. He grabbed hold of the finger and twisted it.

"Now, now!" I said. "No finger-fighting! How about a bit of bike-jousting practice?"

"Yeah! Good idea!" shouted Thurston and Max together. "To the training ground, men!"

We charged through the door and dived on to our binbags.

OK, knights never had bin-bags, but
if you want a fast ride on your belly
down a steep grassy
slope, nothing
beats a
bin-bag.
Wheeee-
oooow!

Normally
Sniff joins in
that kind of fun.
But suddenly he
went skidding down
the other side of the
slope.

"Where's he off to?" said Max, as
Sniff ran three times round The Toot
and shot off into the undergrowth
somewhere.

I whistled but he took no notice. "Must have seen a rabbit or something," I said.

Max was already kitted out, so he was first on his bike with his lance at the ready and his battleaxe in his belt. (It was a mallet really but he said it was a battleaxe.) I had

to get my helmet and breastplate on but I was ready before Thurston. You don't really need leg armour for bike-jousting, but Sir Thirsty thought he looked dead smart in his. "Pass me my *cuisses*," he commanded.

"I'm not your squire!" I said. But I knew he'd take hours if I didn't help him with the straps. They did up at the back like cricket pads. "And don't say you're wearing those pointy shoes! How are you going to pedal?"

"You're just jealous, you varlet!" snapped Sir Thirsty. "No proper knight rides out without his *sabatons*."

Me and Sir Max had made our own lances out of broom handles with boxing gloves on the end.

That wasn't good enough for Sir Thirsty. Being rich and spoiled, he got his dad to buy him all the proper stuff. So his lance was miles longer than ours with a red whirly stripe all along it. It had a built-on fist-protector, and a smart sort of little sandbag to unsaddle your enemies with.

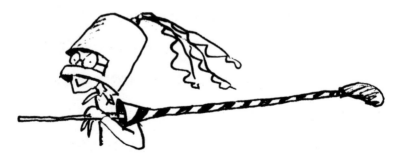

Finally he was ready. "Tally ho!" he screamed and shot off ahead of us down the little track with his lance over his shoulder.

Cheek!

At the Training Ground

The training ground was under
this massive oak tree near the
bottom edge of the wood. There
were cows in the hummocky fields
on the other side of the fence. Years
ago, they must have let them into
the wood. You could tell they'd
nibbled at the branches and
smoothed them off level. It was
wicked, like being under a big
green circus tent.

Sir Benjamin (that's me) and Sir Max got there well ahead of Sir Pointy Boots. He kept getting his lance caught in the branches overhead. And every now and then he got his *sabatons* caught in his front spokes. You could hear them going BRRRRRRRRR!

"Agghhhh! Wait! I've fallen off!" Crash!

"Yessss!" yelled me and Max. "Serves you right!" We raised our broom handles in the air and pedalled ahead of him like crazy.

As soon as we arrived at the training ground, Max panted, "Let's do quarterstaffs first!" He chucked his bike up against the oak and raised his broomstick over his head.

"Have at thee!" I screamed and let my proud steed slide from under me. We bashed away at each other like mad. We were quite good at the criss-cross stuff. That's where you push at each other with two hands in the middle of your weapon. But

it doesn't half hurt when somebody whacks you on the knuckles!

So it wasn't long before we were looking for something else that knights do when they're training.

We did "lifting the heavy stone" for our muscles, but that was boring. Then Thurston finally turned up. He was pushing his bike. He'd left his *sabatons* down the track somewhere and his lance was bust in half. He looked well upset.

"Bad luck, Thurst!" I said. "What happened?"

"Rubbish *thing*!" shrilled Thurston. "I tried pointing it down the path instead of over my shoulder. Trouble is, it won't go round corners and it got caught in a bush! Now it's snapped in two!"

"Let's have a look, see if we can fix it," I said.

"Tell you what," said Max. "Take that fist-guard off it, sharpen up the end and you've got a wicked javelin! Wanna borrow my penknife?"

Maybe Max's brain *is* only the size of half a walnut, but that was a *well* tasty idea!

In no time, Sir Thurston was running round, happy as sandpaper, chucking his "javelin" at rotten logs.

Meanwhile, me and Sir Max were "at the pel". Have you heard of that? It's where you build your wrists up by whacking at a stick – or in our case, a tree trunk – with your mighty sword. That doesn't do plastic swords much good, so we did "sword and buckler" instead. That's where you use your little shield as well as your sword to bash your enemy with. That was a *really* good laugh.

Then we took it in turns to do jousting practice. Did I say about the tyre-swing we had on the oak tree? Well, it came in handy

as a target for your lance. The
idea was, you had to pedal once
round the oak as fast as you could.
You were allowed to keep your
lance steady on the handlebars
while you got up speed. Then you
tucked one end under your arm

and lifted up the boxing-glove end and tried to hit the tyre. Double points if you went through the middle.

It wasn't as easy as it looked. I missed on both my goes. Thurston just managed to graze the outside of the tyre with his javelin.

Of course, Max said we were both rubbish and just watch him. So we did. Annoyingly, he got double points on his first go. I was busy trying to put him off so he would skid on a tree root next time round, and so was Thurston.

That's why we never even noticed the man with a shotgun creeping up behind us.

The Warning

"Hoy, you!" he bellowed.

When you've got a dog like Sniff, you get used to *Hoy, yous*. Still, that doesn't stop you nearly jumping out of your skin when it happens.

When I turned round there was this huge, lopsided man! He had his shirt unbuttoned to the waist under his green tweed jacket. He had curly hairs like brambles sprouting on his chest – and a face like thunder.

25

Mr Bartrum! I realized straight away that his *Hoy, you* wasn't aimed at me. True, he was holding the scruff of a filthy, wet, shivering creature that looked very much like Sniff. Still, he was glaring at Max, not me.

"Is this your mutt, sonny?" growled Mr Bartrum.

"No, Mister B—" It nearly came out *No, Mister Bedroom* but he just managed to turn it into "No, sir" in the nick of time.

26

"Well, that do surprise me," said Mr Bartrum. "Because this mutt ain't wearing no collar, see? And he's up to no good, splashing about in the stream down under the footbridge. After His Lordship's pheasant chicks, he was. So I thought, "Who do I know what gets up to no good and goes after other people's property?" And I put two and two together and it added up to ... you!"

Max's mouth opened and closed like a tortoise trying to get a grip on a lettuce. Finally he came out with, "D-d-did you want to keep that table then?"

"Yes, I *did* want the woodwormy old thing! I wanted it taken down the dump and got rid of properly! So you just put it back on the skip what I paid good money for!"

I could see Sniff was getting nervous so I thought I'd better own up about him. I said,

"Hello, Mr Bartrum, nice day, could I have Sniff back, please?"

He turned his squinty black eyes on me. Like tadpoles, they were, in the shadow of his cloth cap. "Ah. Him's *your* dog, is he? And you're Mr Moore's boy, ain't cher?"

"Yes, Ben Moore," I said.

He looked me up and down, getting more lopsided all the time. "Well, Ben Moore. A knight like you ought to know the rules of who's who and what's what. Don't you know that a gamekeeper is allowed to shoot trespassing dogs chasing birds what belong to a Lord of the Manor? And I shall remind your dad about that. I'm seeing him at The Hall on Monday night at the planning meeting for the Village Show!"

"B-but you said Sniff was under the footbridge," I spluttered. "That's nowhere near Lord Almeley's part of the wood. He was chasing something, that's all.

But we never go through the gate where it says PRIVATE."

"Oh, your dog can *read*, can he?" snarled Mr Bartrum. "Well, I'll tell you what. If he can't read, you'd better learn him quick. Or better still you better keep him out of Batch Wood altogether! Because some nasty sneaking brute has been getting among them birds what I've reared by hand. And when I catch him, he's getting both barrels of this!" He gave his shotgun a shake in Sniff's face. "Now get out of here, the lot of yer! And take that tyre down from that tree before you go!"
Not fair! What a spoilsport!

Found Out

I didn't quite get round to mentioning our meeting with Mr Bartrum to Dad that evening. Mum wasn't too pleased about me drying Sniff off on her bath towel, and I didn't fancy another row.

I just kept my fingers crossed that Mr Bartrum would forget to say anything on Monday night at the planning meeting.

Some hopes!

Dad really had a go at me at breakfast on Tuesday morning.

"So embarrassing!" he moaned.

"He came out with the whole horror story about your gang in front of Lord Almeley and everybody on the committee! Stealing tables! Worrying pheasant chicks!"

My little sister Sal said, "Nah nah, Biggy!" and chucked a piece of eggy bread at me. It missed. SCHHLOPPPP! went Sniff and looked up hopefully for some more.

Fair play to Dad, he did listen to

my side of the story. In the end, I think he even felt a bit sorry for us Knights of the Brown Table. "Gosh, well, he's got no right at all to chuck you out of the woods," he said. "And it was mean of him to make you take down your swing. But it's probably safer to keep right out of his way for the time being. So Batch Wood is off limits – to you and to Hungry Guts there! Is that clear?"

Sniff gave him an adoring look and tried to jump into his lap. Dad shoved him off and mopped up his spilt tea. "So who are we going to get for the Village Show, then?" I said. "The Red Arrows?"

"You wish!" said Dad.

"But we *are* going to get the The Jumpin Jax, aren't we? They were wicked!" I was talking about a boys' motorbike display team. They had them at the Kington Show  the year before. They can jump over cars and everything. Dad had

 promised he'd tell everyone at the meeting they would be a *mega* attraction for our village show. All we normally got was boring old

crafts, plant stalls and donkey rides. They never had anything really *good*.

"Sorry, son," said Dad. "I did my best for you. A lot of people were keen, but Mr Bartrum put his foot down. First of all, he told Lord Almeley that motorbikes would cut up his paddock, even if they weren't full size. His Lordship said that didn't matter, he was used to that with the horses. So what did Mr Bartrum say? He said that the noise would upset the pheasant chicks!"

"But the woods are miles away from Almeley Hall!" I said.

"I know, son!" said Dad. "But you know Lord Almeley – his birds are more important to him than anything."

"Yeah," I muttered. "So important he goes out and shoots them."

"Yes, well," said Dad. "Anyway, what with one thing and another, the highlight of the show this year is …"

"Not that woman with the dancing ducks!" I said. "Not again!"

"Got it in one," said Dad gloomily.

Panic Stations

Next day, I was having a quiet afternoon at home with just Max. I say quiet, but he's useless at computer football games and he's *such* a bad loser. My arm was covered in bruises where he kept punching it.

We were just sneaking downstairs for a game of Hunt the Biscuit Tin. Mum always hides it when Max comes round. I wonder why.

Anyway, thinking of Jammy Dodgers made me think of Sniff.

"I don't beleeeeeve it!" I gasped. "He's gone."

"He's only gone to work," said Max.

"Not DAD, you div!" I hissed. "I'm talking about the dog! He's done a runner! And I've got a horrible feeling he's gone over to Batch Wood!"

"You don't think he's after them peasant chicks, do you?"

"They are *pheasants*, Max. *You're* a peasant. And YES I DO think he's after them! Quick, call Thurst!"

Bee bee bee bah beep, went the phone. "Hail, Sir Thurston! Sir Max here. Drop everythin' and get on your trusty steed quick. We're on a request!"

"A what?" squeaked Thurston's voice at the other end.

"No, you walnut!" I yelled. "Knights go on *quests*, not *re*-quests!" I tried to grab the phone.

"That's what I said, quest!" snarled Max through his teeth as he fought me off. "Get in the saddle, Sir Thirsty, because we are on a quest to save a helpless doggy from a fire-breathing shotgun!"

The Quest

We all met up outside the paper shop. We were in pretty good spirits at first. It was only when we were pedalling up the hill towards the top end of Batch Wood that we really started to think about what we might be getting into.

"It's not just your stupid dog that's in the firing line," complained Thurston, pushing back his visor so that he could see where he was going. "It's us as well."

"Tell me about it!" I said. "If Dad finds out I'm off limits, he's going to ground me till Christmas!"

"Mr Bedroom's *deferably* gonna shoot me," moaned Max. "I still haven't put the table back on the skip."

We pulled up just by the dirt track that drops into the woods. Our hearts were thumping, I can tell you.

looked at one another, hoping
that somebody would come up with
a way out of this mess. It was so
quiet it was spooky.

Suddenly the silence got ripped
to shreds. "RAAAALPH! RAAAALPH!
AYEEEEEEE! EEE! EEE!"

"Sniff!" I said. "I'd know that bark
anywhere! And he does that whiny
howl at the end when he's really
excited about something!"

"It's coming from right over
there!" said Thurston, pointing
towards Lord Almeley's end of the
woods. "Don't say he's got into the
pens where the pheasant chicks are!"

He swivelled his bike round and
flipped a pedal up. "Where are you
going?" I said. "You're not going to

leave me and Max, are you?"

"Oh, you think it's sensible to hang about, do you?" snapped Thurston. "Mr Bartrum's bound to come running when he hears that barking!"

"But we're the Knights of the Brown Table!" I reminded him. "Go on Max, tell him what our motto is."

I was hoping he'd say "One for all and all for Sniff!" but Max went blank. Then he said,

"Oh I know!" he grinned, raising his trusty battleaxe. *"One gets killed, we all get killed!"*

Thurston nearly fell off his bike laughing. "How the heck did I get myself into this mob?" he giggled. "All right, Sir Benjamin, giveth us our orders!"

"Stick with me and don't get caught," I commanded.

In the Firing Line

The barking got louder and more frantic as we approached the sign by the five-bar gate that said:

PRIVATE. Game Rearing Area. No Public Access.

"He's *deferably* in there, *deferably*," whispered Max.

"Tell us something we *don't* know," said Thurston.

"Hush, you two," I said. "I'll try whistling him." I put my finger and thumb under my tongue and let go an ear-splitter.

The barking stopped dead.

"He heard it," said Max.

The barking started up again only louder and with more whining on the end.

"Yeah, and he's not taken a blind bit of notice!" complained Thurston. "I bet he's going MAD! He's probably chasing chicks round the pen biting heads off left right and centre!"

"Come on," I said, "we've got to get him out of here!" and hopped over the gate.

The others followed and we

ducked down and ran more like commandoes than knights towards the noise. We bashed through ferns and bushes, too scared to notice the brambles that tore at our ankles and wrists.

"There are the pens!" I croaked and threw myself down, dragging Max and Thurston with me.

We lifted our heads just high enough to peek at them. They were like those low cages you put on the lawn for your guinea pigs, with chicken wire on the top and sides.

"Can't see any chicks," whispered Max.

"I just hope they've run for cover into their hutches," I said.

"There he is!" squeaked Thurston, grabbing my arm. "Over there!" We tried to follow where his finger was pointing but the sun was getting lower and somehow it made the shady parts of the wood even darker.

"Don't say he's got inside one of the pens!" I gasped.

"No, over there, look. Standing

with his front legs up on that beech tree."

Just as I saw him, there was a snapping noise that made his head spin round and made us all jump. It sounded for a second like a heavy man standing on a dry stick. But it was even worse than that!

By instinct we leapt to our feet and waved our swords and battleaxe in the air.

It was stupid, because the noise we heard wasn't a stick snapping.

It was the sound of Mr Bartrum
snapping his shotgun shut. He was
lining up the loaded chambers of
the twin barrels with the twin firing-
hammers! Slowly, he raised the gun
to his shoulder and aimed both
barrels at Sniff.

"NOOOOO!" howled the Knights
of the Brown Table.

Caught Red-Pawed

There was a mighty crack!

"AHHH!" screamed the Knights of the Brown Table as we dived for cover.

But this time it really was the sound of a heavy bloke standing on a dry stick!

"HOY YOU!" yelled Mr Bartrum. He meant everybody in the village by the sound of it. For some reason Sniff stood exactly where he was, standing on his back legs with his front paws up a beech tree.

"Don't shoot Sniff, please Mr Bartrum," I yelled back. "It's not his fault!"

"Idiots!" shouted Mr Bartrum. "You could all have been blown to smithereens! And as for that blasted dog, he deserves to be shot. He's been worrying my birds all week! He's lifted the wire on three of the pens, look!"

"It wasn't him," said Max in a surprisingly steady voice. "It was a different animal altogether!"

"Shut up, Max," I said out of the corner of my mouth. He was in enough trouble with Mr Bartrum already without trying to be clever now!

But Max stood firm. "Well what's that, then?" he challenged, and pointed up the tree. Thurston gave his glasses a wipe on his chain mail and squashed them back on to his face. "Christmas Crackers!" he yelled. "Max is right. Look on that branch! It's a black and white cat!"

"Fooffy!" sobbed Mr Bartrum.

"You've come back to me! I thought you were gone for good!"

"You don't mean to say that's *your* pussy cat, Mr Bartrum?" said Max.

"He's been gone for a week! I – I thought he must have got run over or something!" gasped Mr Bartrum. "Oh the poor thing! He must be terrified! How's he going to get down from there?"

"Give us a leg up," said Max to the lopsided gamekeeper. "Ben, hold on to Sniff."

It took Max about five minutes to capture Fooffy and lower him into the arms of his delighted owner.

Meanwhile Thurston had been

doing a bit of detective work among the pens. "Look what I found caught on the chicken wire here!" he crowed. He held up a tuft of black and white hair for us all to see. "So there's no doubt about who was the real chick-worrier!"

"Elementary, my dear Sir Thurston!" I said. "Tut, tut, Fooffy!"

"Quest over!" grinned Sir Max.

Sniff had been lying down with his nose between his front paws,

looking a bit sorry for himself.
I tapped him on the shoulders
with my sword.

"Rise, Sir Sniff," I said.

A Few Surprises

It was quite understandable that
Mr Bartrum didn't want this story to
get back to Lord Almeley.

It wasn't too surprising that Max
was allowed to hang on to his
precious brown table. Us knights
were invited to muck about in Batch
Woods any time we liked, but no
surprise there either.

What *was* surprising was that when
we went to put the tyre-swing back

in the oak tree, we found that *somebody* had rigged up this dead good rope ladder. And when you climbed up to see what was on the platform above, there were three long-bows and a whole bundle of home-made arrows with proper feathers. There was a note saying,

"A Big Ta from Fooffy."

But the best thing of all was when Dad came home the following Monday night after the next planning meeting for the Village Show. He'd bought a poster that Lady Almeley had designed.

"It was Mr Bartrum's idea! Brilliant, eh?" said Dad, scratching his head.

**Grand Village Show
At Almeley Hall**

featuring

𝔄 𝔐𝔢𝔡𝔦𝔢𝔳𝔞𝔩 𝔗𝔬𝔲𝔯𝔫𝔞𝔪𝔢𝔫𝔱 𝔞𝔫𝔡 𝔍𝔢𝔞𝔰𝔱

Boys in armour FREE!

"Funny, I thought he was a just a mean old spoilsport!"

The hairs on Sniff's scruff stood up suddenly. He growled, whined and threw himself at the patio doors.

"It's next door's cat scratching up my prize carrots!" grumbled Dad. "See him off, boy!"

"Raaalph!" said Sir Sniff. Just the sort of quest he liked!

Collect them all! Why not try these other **Books for Boys**:

Robin Hood's Best Shot

A Footballer Called Flip

There's a Spell up my Nose

Boy Racer

Aliens Stole my Dog

The Boy who had (nearly) Everything

Alex, the Walking Accident

Through the Cat-Flap

The Secret Superhero

If you have enjoyed reading about Sniff, look out for more Sniff stories by Ian Whybrow:

Sniff
Sniff Bounces Back
Nice One, Sniff
Sniff the Wonderdog

"I laughed aloud, not once, but lots of times …" *TES*